Berner Bane Finds His Family

By
Winston & Julia Smith

ISBN: 9798706451059 (Paperback)

First paperback edition February 2021.

Edited by Winston & Julia Smith
Cover art by Yani Agustina
Illustrations by Yani Agustina
Layout by Winston & Julia Smith

Published by Transatlantic Digital Media Limited
Toronto, Canada

www.BernerBane.com

This book is dedicated to
our wonderful Bernese Mountain Dog

Bane

You have filled our life with
immeasurable joy…

…even when you eat our shoes.

Today was a special day at Friendly Dog Farms because today was Puppy Picking Day.

All of the puppies jumped up and down with excitement. They could not wait to meet their new families.

That is, all but one...

...Berner Bane

Bane was a Bernese Mountain Dog.

They were known for being strong, brave and very very big.

But Berner Bane was not. He was a runt, which made him weak, shy and small.

And because he was different, he thought that no family would ever pick him.

What Berner Bane and the other puppies
did not know was that he was special.

Although Bane was the smallest.
he had the biggest heart.
His heart was so big that he could make
even the saddest person smile.

As the puppies prepared to meet the families,
they licked their fur and feet clean.

Berner Bane sat alone and stared out the window.

He saw all of the happy families outside
and wished with all his heart that
one day he could find a family too.

"Haha!" Poppy the Toy Poodle said.
"No one will ever pick you! You are too small to be a Bernese Mountain Dog
and too big to be a city dog."

"Leave him alone Poppy"
said Memphis the Husky.

"He is a good dog,
he is only a little small...
that's all."

"Don't worry about it,
you will find a family Ban
said Murray the old Mast

Poppy the Toy Poodle sat up and began to walk towards Bane.

She whispered in his ear "If you want to get picked you need to act like a real dog."

Berner Bane knew what Poppy said was true.
He did not look like a 'normal' Bernese Mountain Dog.

Berner Bane let out a sigh, and carefully watched
the families approach the barn. He saw their smiling faces
and began to smile too.

His heart filled with bittersweet emotions as they began to enter through
the big barn doors.

As they entered one by one, Memphis began to run back and forth around the barn.
Quick as lightning he bounced off every wall displaying his Husky speed
to the crowd of people.

Puzzled and interested by what he saw, Berner Bane tilted his head left and right.
He soon realised that this is what Poppy meant by being a 'real dog'.

Bane now knew what he had to do...

He had to show the people that he could run just as fast as
Memphis the Husky, that he was a 'real dog' too.

Berner Bane was not very good at running.
As a Bernese Mountain Dog,
his legs were built for climbing mountains and
not for running at high speed like a Husky.

But right now, the only thing that Berner Bane wanted was a family,
so no matter what he would try his best to be a 'real dog.'

Round and round in circles they ran, knocking down stools and kicking up the straw and dust that covered the Barn floor.

As the dust filled the room and coated his amber eyes,
Berner Bane could not see a thing.

He was not sure if he was being noticed by the families,
but he knew he would not give up.

All of a sudden, he heard a little girl say loudly,

"That one! That one! I want that one!".

As the straw settled on the Barn floor,
Berner Bane's eyes were teary with dust.

He squinted and saw the outline of
the farmer hobble towards him
with arms outstretched.

Filled with excitement Berner Bane wagged
his tail in anticipation. Ready to be scooped up by
the farmer and meet his family.
This was it.
This was Berner Bane's moment to be picked.

"I told you that you needed to act like a real dog." Poppy said.

"At this rate, you will never be picked by a family."

Poppy strolled confidently towards the potential puppy parents.

"Watch and learn" she scoffed at Berner Bane.

She sat quietly in front of the crowd of people.
She looked up at them with her moon-like eyes
batting her eyelashes.

An old grandmother emerged from the group of people.
"Oh, aren't you the most beautiful little girl? You are perfect!"
said the grandmother to Poppy.

She picked up Poppy and walked out of the barn door.

One by one the young dogs that Berner Bane had spent
his puppyhood with all began to disappear,
only to realize that he was
one of the last puppies left on the farm.

"Dont give up kid."

YELP!

Bane's heart sank as he lost hope
of finding his own family.

"Don't give up kid" said Murray the old Mastiff.
Bane forced a smile but inside his big Berner heart was breaking.
All he had ever wanted was a family of his own.
As Berner Bane sat near the window watching the world pass him
by he was interrupted by a loud "Yelp!" from the outside...

He jumped down from the window and began to sprint out the barn door.

As he emerged from the barn, he saw his friend Nala crying on the ground. Nala had fallen from the arms of its new owner and had hurt its paw.

Berner Bane dashed across the driveway towards Nala.

At that moment, Bane was no longer worried about finding a family.

The only thing in his big Berner heart was making sure that Nala was okay.

With his little pink tongue, Berner Bane began to lick Nala's injured paw.

As soon as Bane licked her paw, Nala began to smile
and hop around in circles, smiling back at Berner Bane.

Out of nowhere, a young couple picked Bane up and held him in their arms. Bane felt a warm and fuzzy feeling wash over him as the strange man and woman cradled him.

"We would like to bring him home, what is his name?" the young man said to the farmer.

The farmer looked at them and smiled,
"His name is Bane."

"Berner Bane, you have the biggest heart of all…"
said the woman as she looked into Berner Bane's eyes.

They piled into the car together,
Bane's big heart swelled with joy.
He had finally found his family.

Berner Bane had finally understood
what it meant to be a 'real dog'...

...he only had to be himself.